The Monsters

in

Birthday Mud Hunt

Scholastic Children's Books,
Scholastic Publications Ltd,
7-9 Pratt Street, London NW1 0AE, UK

Scholastic Inc.,
730 Broadway, New York, NY 10003, USA

Scholastic Canada Ltd,
123 Newkirk Road, Richmond Hill,
Ontario, Canada L4C 3G5

Ashton Scholastic Pty Ltd,
PO Box 579, Gosford, New South Wales,
Australia

Ashton Scholastic Ltd,
Private Bag 1, Penrose, Auckland,
New Zealand

First published by Scholastic Publications Ltd, 1994

ISBN: 0 590 55594 4

Typeset by Rapid Reprographics, London
Printed and bound in Belgium by Proost Book Production

10 9 8 7 6 5 4 3 2 1

The Monsters

in

Birthday Mud Hunt

Frank Rodgers

Monsters love mud.

They love to play with it...

they love
to slide on it...

they love to paddle in it...

and they even like to eat it!

In the swamp where they live there are pools of a special kind of Monster mud that all Monsters think is delicious!

They eat lots of Monster mud cakes at parties.
Especially birthday parties!

"We're going to make you an enormous mud cake for your birthday party today," said Ring-tailed Monster's friends.

"Faburiffic!" cried Ring-tailed Monster.
"I love birthday mud cakes!"

But when the Monsters looked into the big baskets where they kept the delicious Monster mud, they were disappointed. There was none left!

"No time to lose!" cried Long-horned Monster. "Ring-tailed Monster's party starts soon so we must go and find some Monster mud."

Quickly everyone grabbed an empty basket and set off on the birthday mud hunt.

Unfortunately the Monsters weren't very good at finding things.

They searched high...

and they
searched
low...

but they couldn't find a pool of delicious Monster mud anywhere.

"Oh dear," sighed Curly-top Monster, "that means Ring-tailed Monster won't have a cake."

"I don't mind," said Ring-tailed Monster.

"But we do," said her friends. "You must have a cake."

"Why don't we climb to the top of that big hill and look around," suggested Furry Monster.

"Good idea!" exclaimed the others, and everyone set off at once, clambering and scrambling up the side of the high hill.

But when they got to the top they still couldn't see any pools of delicious Monster mud.

"I wish we could go higher still," said Curly-top Monster. "We would get a better view."

"Why don't we build a tower with our baskets," suggested Short-horned Monster. "Then we could climb to the top and look around."

"That's another good idea!" gasped the Monsters. "Two today. That's a record for us!"

Quickly, they piled up their baskets, one on top of the other...

and in no time at all they had built a look-out tower.

"Who's going to climb up?" asked Long-horned Monster.

"Perhaps no one should," replied Short-horned Monster. "It looks too wobbly."

The words were no sooner out of his mouth when suddenly there was a great gust of wind...

which blew the wobbly tower of baskets high
into the air.

The Monsters watched in dismay as the wind
swept their baskets out over the tree-tops
and down out of sight.

"This is not a mud hunt any more," wailed Hairy
Monster. "It's a basket hunt!"

"They landed behind those trees!" chorused the Spotted Monsters.

"Then let's go over there and look for them," suggested Furry Monster, and everyone dashed back down the hill.

Again they searched high and they searched low.

But their baskets were nowhere to be found.

Suddenly, Ring-tailed Monster pointed. "There they are!" she cried excitedly.

Everyone looked. Sure enough, there they were, lying in a heap just through the trees.

"Now we can get on with our Monster mud hunt!" yelled the Monsters gleefully and rushed off to get their baskets.

Ring-tailed Monster was the quickest and got there first.

But she was running so fast that she couldn't stop. CRASH! She disappeared under the pile of baskets.

When the others arrived, Ring-tailed Monster still hadn't come out.

They peered into the darkness beneath the baskets. "Yoo hoo!" they called. "Are you in there?"

Up popped Ring-tailed Monster, all muddy and licking her lips.

"Happy Birthday to me!" she sang.

"Our baskets landed on top of a pool of delicious Monster mud!"

"Faburiffic!" cried her friends. "The birthday mud hunt is over!"

And they all dived under the baskets to get a taste.

The Monsters each brought back a brimming basket full of Monster mud.

"Now we can make an enormous mud cake for Ring-tailed Monster's birthday," they said.

And that's what they did.

But not only did they make a mud cake, they made mud-covered doughnuts, mud pies, mud biscuits, mud shakes and even mud jelly!

"That was the best birthday mud hunt ever!"
laughed Ring-tailed monster.

And everyone agreed.